THE BLESSING OF ANIMALS

The Blessing of Animals

LAURAINE SNELLING

The Blessing of Animals
© 2020 by Lauraine Snelling. All rights reserved

Published in association with the Books & Such Literary Management, 52 Mission Circle, Suite 122, PMB 170, Santa Rosa, CA 95409-5370, www.booksandsuch.com.

Scripture Quotations are from the King James Version of the Bible. All characters and events in this book are fictitious. Any resemblance to actual persons, living or dead, or to actual events is purely coincidental.

All rights reserved. No part of this publication may be reproduced, stored in a retrieval system, or transmitted in any form or by any means—electronic, mechanical, photocopy, recording or any other—except for brief quotations in printed reviews without the written prior permission of the publisher.

ISBN: 9798617800663

Printed in the United States of America

15 14 13 12 10 9 8 7 6 5 4 3 2 1

TABLE OF CONTENTS

A Letter to Readers · 1
The Darkest Night · 3
When Stubborn Meets Stubborn · 16
Angel In Gold Fur · 22
When Heigh Ho Silver Came to Our House · · · · · · · · · · · · · · 37
Chewey · 44
Dogs Know · 49
Wolf to the Rescue · 52

Dear Readers,

Through the years I have written various animal stories, some are true life experiences and others are fiction. As you who have read other books of mine know, I have animals of one kind or another in every book I have written, dogs, cats, horses, cows, mules, oxen, although they've never had more than a working part, buffalo, elephants, chickens and pigs and a wolf. Some are part of the story, some star in the story. Putting this book together has made me want to write more, both about animals in my life and animal characters in fiction. BTW, George the Buffalo from the Wild West Wind series has a special place in my heart. And the elephants in *Streams of Mercy* showed up because of a dare.

I hope you enjoy all of these stories and you can count on more coming, just not sure when.

Blessings,
Lauraine

The Darkest Night

"Robby... Robby!"

My voice cracked. Tension crept over the top of my scalp and pulled at my eyes. Where had he gone? I had put my three-year-old, not-so-charming-today son to bed for his usual one o'clock nap. He and I both needed it after the fussy morning we'd had. Nothing had gone right. Panic was giving me the shakes.

It started off when Bob and I had an argument-no, not an argument, a fight. Money again-the fights were always over money. I hate to send my husband off to work with angry words. I guess everyone woke up in a cranky mood.

"Robby, where are you?" I looked in the beds, the closets, all over the house. Where would such a little tyke go?

I dialed my neighbor and best friend. "Marge!" My voice rose an octave. "Robby is gone. Have you seen him?"

"Now, calm down," Marge said in her soft-spoken way.

Who wants to be calm? I want to see Robby-now!

"How long has he been gone?"

"I don't know. I put him down at one like always, but I was still so tired from that flu I had I had to lay down for a nap. I only meant to sleep half an hour, but I didn't wake up. Now... he's gone."

"Where have you looked?"

"Everywhere... the house... the yard. He's never opened the gate by himself before."

"I'll get my coat. The kids will be home from school in a couple of minutes. They can help us look."

"Hurry!" I hung up, but my fingers clung to the phone.

Pulse racing, I glanced around my yellow and orange kitchen; the breakfast table not yet cleared, our tiger cat licking up the milk Robby had spilled at lunch. When would I get my act together? Morning fights made me feel like chucking it all, like I was completely worthless.

I shook my head. Who cares about that? Right now, Robby was all that mattered. *Think, Pat, think!*

A gust of late October chill blew in as Marge opened the back door. There's nothing like late fall in Washington state to put goosebumps on your arms.

"Brrr. Let's go." She paused. "Have you called Bob yet?"

"No, I'm afraid to. He left in such a huff this morning. He'll just think this is one more thing I can't do right."

"Call him. He needs to know."

"No, I can't. We'll find Robby any minute. It's no use worrying him for nothing." I tried to smile. That's all it would take, a few minutes. After all, a little guy like Robby couldn't have gone far.

Shrieks and hollers of "good-bye" and "see you tomorrow" rang from the long yellow school bus stopped in front of Marge's house. She dashed out the front door.

"You kids drop your stuff. Robby is gone. Help us look for him."

Bashful, sixteen-year-old Kevin was the first to run around to our back door. "Gosh, Pat, I-I'm sorry. Have you looked in the woods yet?"

"No, he's never gone outside the fence before."

"Where's Blacky?" Kevin glanced over at the empty chain in front of the dog house.

"I don't know." I hadn't thought to check. "Wait, Blacky was in the house." I thought back. "I let him off the chain this morning so he and Robby could play inside. It was so cold out."

I started to shiver again. Marge put her arms around my shoulders.

"Kevin, go look in the woods, down by the creek. If Robby is with Blacky-well you know how that dog loves water."

"Where do you want me to go, Mom?" asked Karen, Kevin's graceful blond twin. The twins took turns sitting for Robby on the rare nights we went out. Kevin had been teaching Robby how to catch a football. Karen read him stories by the hour. They both treated him like a much loved baby brother.

"Down the street, check at each of the houses. Maybe they went into someone else's back yard to play."

Both kids took off. "Now, you go up the street that way," Marge said to me, "and I'll go over one block and cover Garfield," She waved as she jogged across the newly patched asphalt.

I nodded. It was all I could do. While the sun was shining, the late afternoon sun tugged at my sheepskin jacket. I wondered if Robby had on a jacket. I'd forgotten to check.

I mounted my bike with the youth carrier bolted on the back.

"Robby... *Robby!*" I called again and again. "Blacky!" I tried to whistle. My lips wouldn't pucker. Robby and Blacky must be together, or Blacky would have come by now. He never left Robby by himself. From the start, he had been Robby's self-appointed guardian.

I rang every doorbell.

"Have you seen a little boy, three years old with curly brown hair, blue eyes? He's with a large black lab." If no one answered, I looked in the backyard anyway. My voice sounded like I'd spent three hours cheering at a close basketball game.

What was he wearing? So hard to remember. *Blue jeans. He always wears those. I think I got out a red t-shirt for him this morning.*

At the end of the pavement the houses quit too. A large grassy field sloped down to tall evergreens.

I turned and pedaled for home. Maybe one of the others had had more luck than I. That's it. Robby would be sitting at the kitchen table. Kevin would be tickling him 'til he squirmed. And Marge would fix us all a cup of cocoa.

The tree blocks back to the house seemed to take forever. No lights in the front room, they'd all be in the kitchen. I opened the door to silence. The mess was still there, but no Robby.

"Oh God, please watch over him. He's so little."

Marge and Karen came running in the back door.

"No sign of them," Marge panted. "I went up and down both sides of Garfield. No one had seen them."

"I went clear down to the shopping center," Karen added. "Nothing."

"Has Kevin come back yet?" Marge asked.

"Don't think so, but I just got back myself. How far can a little guy go?"

Karen shrugged, her lips quivering.

I grabbed Marge's hands. "You don't suppose someone kidnapped him?"

"No." She squeezed my cold hands. "No, Blacky wouldn't let that happen. No one touches Robby when he's around!" Marge, always the logical one. Thank you, God, for a friend like her.

"Where can I go next?" Karen's blue eyes filled with tears. Karen often came over to take Robby with her on walks.

"Why don't you hit the woods and help Kevin? There's a lot of ground to cover back there."

"Guess I'd better call Bob." I hunched my shoulders.

"Yes, and the police right after that. We've got to have more help."

I could hardly see the numbers as I dialed the phone.

"Can I speak to Bob Hansen, please?" I could hear the compressors in the background. The paint sprayers at Bob's body shop were always busy.

"Pat, you know I've asked you not to call me at work."

I interrupted him. "Bob, it's an emergency. Robby's gone."

"Gone? What do you mean gone?"

"I can't find him anywhere. Marge and the kids and I have been looking all over. We can't find him."

"Is Blacky with him?"

"Must be, he's not here either."

"Have you called the police?"

"No, I'm going to call right away. Marge said to call you first. Bob, it's getting dark and cold...and...and I'm so scared." I started to cry.

"Calm down, Pat. Call the police. I'll be there as soon as I can."

I hung up the phone and leaned against the wall, trying to stop the tears that had turned into hiccups. Marge wrapped both arms around me. What if I had been all alone? I had never appreciated her calm assurance and good sense more than now.

She shoved a cup of coffee into my hands. "Drink this and tell me what Bob said."

"He'll be home as soon as he can. Now I have to make sure about what Robby is wearing and call the police. I'll check his bedroom. You look in the living room. See if his blue jacket is anywhere."

I stopped at the door to Robby's room. The bedcover was rumpled, as if he had just climbed out of it, his white-tummied teddy bear thrown against the wall. The red fire truck-how I tired of hearing that clanging bell-was parked in the center of the Big Bird rug. No jacket anywhere. There were his tennis shoes...oh, dear heaven...his tennis shoes. What did he have on his feet?

I ran to the kitchen where the jackets and boots lines one wall by the pantry. *Thank you, Jesus, his cowboy boots are gone. No jacket, so he must have that on, too.*

"No jacket in the other room." Marge had come back from her search. "I'll dial 9-1-1. You sit down for a minute." She handed me the telephone.

I slumped against the hard frame of the wooden chair. The wood pressing at the back of my neck helped me concentrate on what to tell the officer.

"Dispatch. How may I help you?"

I clutched the phone. "This is Pat Hansen. My little boy, Robby, is missing." I tried to stifle the sobs but failed.

"Easy now, ma'am. What is your address?"

"336 Hawthorne Lane."

"Phone number?"

"What has that got to do with it? We've got to find Robby!"

"Just give me your phone number," the reassuring voice continued. "I have to know how to get in touch with you. I'll need a lot of information."

"It's 480-3132. Please do something."

"Now tell me exactly about your little boy-"

"Robby."

"What Robby looks like and what he is wearing."

"He is three years old. He has light brown hair-it's curly-and blue eyes. He's wearing…" I continued with the description. It had nothing to do with hugs at bedtime, peanut-butter-and-jelly kisses and soapy giggles in the bathtub. I wondered vaguely how to describe Robby's look of wonder at a tiny tree frog's feet on the front window, his explosion of joy when Blacky puts one paw on Robby's tummy when they wrestle… and licks his face all over.

Robby, the child I get impatient with, but would die without…

I jerked my mind back. "He has on a blue jacket and cowboy boots. Our dog is with him."

"The dog, what does it look like?"

"Blacky is a large black Labrador with a red collar. His license is on the collar."

"Where are some places he likes to play?" The dispatcher continues the questions as I stuttered answers. "How long has he been gone?"

"I missed him at 3:30." The guilt rolled over me like huge breakers. If only I had been more careful, not gone to sleep. My father always said I'd lose my head if it wasn't tacked on. He was right, only it wasn't my head I'd lost. It was his only grandson.

"Has he ever done this before?"

"No, of course not." What did he think? That Robby was a runaway?

"Now, I want you to stay there so someone is always by the phone in case he is found. We'll put officers on this immediately and contact you later."

"Th-th-tank you." Hanging up the wall phone felt like lifting an eighty-pound weight. Nothing on my body worked right. All my eyes wanted to do was run like downspouts in a storm. I wanted to hear a small voice call, "Mommy!" Was it only this morning I had wanted to be left alone for a while? For a long while?

A car door slammed at the same time gravel sprayed from car wheels in the driveway. Bob burst through the back door.

"Have you found him?"

I shook my head as I ran to the comfort of his strong arms. Neither of us said anything for a moment. All of our morning anger disappeared in our need to hold each other.

"Tell me what's happened so far," Bob said.

I told him everything we had done. As I spoke, the tears refused to stay back.

"Bob, I want him home. You know how frightened he must be?"

"I know. Have the twins come back?"

"No." Marge handed Bob a cup of coffee. "I heard them calling him a while ago, but nothing lately."

"Kevin knows those woods as well as anyone. If Robby is with Blacky, that's probably where they are." Bob swallowed the rest of his coffee. "I'm going to find Kevin. You stay here like the officer said."

"But, Bob, I need to be doing something. I'm going out of my mind." Fear tore at my middle again.

Bob hugged me, then shrugged into his sheepskin jacket. "We'll find him, Pat. He's okay."

I looked at the clock: 5:30. Two hours had gone by and no Robby. I stepped out the back door. The sun was down, the woods beyond our cedar fence already darker than dusk. We'd bought this house because of the open fields and woods, such a perfect place for our future children to grow up. No close neighbors gawking in our back window.

Now the majestic evergreens and flaming vine maple were not the rustling friends of our many walks. The star-flung night was our enemy.

I turned and stumbled over the door frame. My feet didn't want to obey. Each minute hung around like an unwelcome salesman.

The doorbell rang. I hurried through the house, hoping to see... but it was only a blue uniform.

"Mrs. Hansen?"

"Yes, won't you come in?"

"We've looked all over the neighborhood. There's a unit out in the woods and information has gone out to all cars." The young officer paused. "I'm sorry, we're doing all we can."

"I know you are. Thank you."

"Is there any more information you can give us? Did he have any medical problems?"

"No, none. He was... is... perfectly healthy." What was my mind doing? *Was.* What an awful thing to think! *I know he is alive. Is. Is, not was.*

"The sheriff's patrol has canine corps. The dog will be here pretty soon. Can you get some clothing your boy has worn recently that you haven't washed?"

My mind kept wandering away from the conversation. *Careless! You are always losing things: car keys, notes, W-2 forms. You are just careless! Now you've really done it!* The voice in my head wouldn't stop.

"Mrs. Hansen, are you listening to me?" The officer touched my shaking arm.

"Um, I think so." I swallowed and wet my lips. "No, I'm sorry, what did you say?"

"Do you have someone here with you?"

"Yes, my neighbor."

He seemed relieved. "Good, we'll be back shortly." He turned to go. "I'm sorry, Mrs. Hansen. I have a little boy too."

Sorry. How can people really know what sorry is? It's not their only baby who is missing.

"Pat...Pat." Marge shook me back a moment. "The canine unit is here. Get something for the dog to smell."

I ran back to Robby's room: the toys were still in the same places. Grabbing his blue gingham baby quilt, I didn't stop to pick up the bereft brown teddy bear that had tumbled to the floor.

All of my friends had embroidered squares for this quilt and then sewn them together for this long-awaited child. Robby loved it and still slept with it, faded though it was. Whenever Robby needed a hug, he'd go get his quilt and pull my leg until I picked him up. Then we'd sit down in the rocker to snuggle.

In the backyard stood several men in the beige uniforms of the local sheriff's department. A large black and tan hound with long ears and sad eyes was straining at a leash. Nose to the ground, he sniffed at all the places where Robby usually played-the sandbox with the red roof in the corner, the blue-and-white swing set. I handed the man the quilt.

"May I take this along?" he asked.

"Yes, it's Robby's." I prayed that the dog would be the one to find Robby.

The sheriff turned back. "By the way, if you hear one shot, it means we found him. A second shot will mean he is okay."

The dog's wet nose had left a streak of mud on the quilt. Dog pulling at the leash, nose to the ground, man and beast left the yard.

I turned back inside, shivering. Beyond chilly. The temperature was dropping fast. The weatherman's prediction for a temperature drop was coming true. Could such a little boy survive in cold like this?

"Pat wake up." I jolted as Bob gently shook me.
"Have you found him? Where's Robby?" I jumped out of the rocker. I couldn't even remember sitting down.
"No, everyone is still looking. I came back for some coffee and something to eat. Have you eaten?"
Food. How could anyone eat at a time like this? My stomach heaved at the smell of chicken noodle soup wafting from the kitchen. I could hear the twins talking with Marge. I felt like I was drifting in another world, looking at this one from far, far away.
"Oh." I sank back into the chair. My legs refused to hold me up.
"Pat, come and have a cup of coffee with me." Bob took my hand and pulled me into the comfort of his arms. I held on to his shoulders, wanting to cry-but all the tears had been used up.
"All right. What time is it?"
"Eleven o'clock."
"Elevin o'clock. Robby's been gone over seven hours." It seemed more like seven days.
"I know. Come on."
"Well," said Marge as the door slammed behind the twins, whom she'd send home to bed, "how about some coffee? Soup? I've got it all hot in case anyone comes back and needs it."
Practical Marge. Always caring for someone else. What a blessing. The kitchen, all clean and shiny, was proof that *she* hadn't been daydreaming.
The night dragged on. Bob went out again about midnight. Each time people came back, I flew to let them in. But each time, no Robby. Where could one little boy have gone in such a short time? How far could he walk? Where was our dog? Blacky should be barking like crazy.
At 4 A.M. the sheriff came in, stamping his feet.

"It'll be dawn soon and easier to locate him. We keep hearing a dog bask every once in a while, but can't zero in on it. Might be one of the neighborhood animals barking at all the commotion." Marge handed him a steaming mug. "Thanks."

"How cold is it out there?" I asked.

"Thirty-five degrees, ma'am. But at least there's no wind or rain." The sheriff had a hard time looking me in the eye. I knew he was losing hope.

"We're giving the dog a rest. We'll take him back out at first light." The man turned to go. "We're doing our best, folks."

I hugged both my elbows with nearly numb hands. I felt so cold here in my house-what about Robby? Being frightened would lower his body temperature even more. I now understood the adage "scared to death."

At five o'clock Bob stumbled back in face drawn and gray. As he collapsed into the nearest chair, I dished him up some soup.

"He's so little..." That's all Bob could say.

I rubbed the back of his neck, the cold from his jacket creeping into my hands. At least he hadn't accused me of carelessness. I was doing enough of that myself. *If only* was such a vicious accuser. It kept buzzing in my mind like a dentist's drill. *If only* I could turn it off.

The other side of my mind kept praying, *God, please bring him back. I'll be more careful. I'll never be impatient with him or anyone again.*

By six the sky had lightened outside the kitchen window. Slowly the fence became visible and then the trees. I heard the patrol head out with the dog in the lead.

A new day; what would it bring? I didn't think I could stand the agony much longer. They had to find him. He had to be *alive*. Death had already come to our house once before, taking our unborn baby girl. Surely it wouldn't happen again. We were much too young. Death was for old people, for other families.

"He's got to be alive!" I nearly screamed the words. Bob stared into his soup mug.

"Easy, Pat. Hang on." Marge hugged me. "Nobody's given up yet." I clung to her. She stayed so positive. Surely God wouldn't let this happen to us.

I stepped out onto the back porch. To the east, pink and vermillion slashed the horizon. Shivers instantly started in my shoulders and engulfed me. It was so cold...so bone-chilling cold.

In the distance I could hear the dog tracking. So different from a regular bark, his voice carried clearly on the early morning breeze.

In an instant the bugling changed, became more frenzied, then steadied to a deep repetition. Bob bounded to the open door.

"He found something. That's his treeing call!" Bob hugged my shoulders, straining to catch any differences in tone.

Standing there shivering, afraid to breathe in case we might miss something, we heard a rifle fire once. They'd found him! I couldn't suck air past the granite boulder in my chest. *God, please, please.* Then another shot...

Robby was alive!

With tears cascading down my cheeks, I turned to Bob and his reassuring arms. Robby was alive; he was coming home to us again.

Half an hour later a beaming sheriff pushed open the gate, holding a grubby little boy in his arms and escorted closely by a black lab.

"Here you are, folks. One tired little fellow."

"Mommy!" Robby reached out to my waiting arms.

Mommy. What a wonderful word. I clutched him close, and Bob hugged us both. Blue eyes sparkled above tear-stained cheeks.

"Mommy, I'm hungry." Robby looked from face to face as we all burst out laughing.

"Leave it to a boy." Marge covered her tears with a chuckle.

Blacky leapt around our feet, not wanting to be left out. We all trooped into the kitchen. After changing his wet clothes, I set Robby in his high chair and took the cereal down from the cupboard.

"Excuse me, folks," the officer interrupted. "I have to file a report. I'll be right back."

The officer later told us they found Blacky and Robby curled up in a narrow ravine under thick huckleberry bushed. He figured Robby had slid down and couldn't climb back out. Robby was still asleep, but Blacky's barking had brought the searchers. Oure faithful dog had curled around Robby's sleeping body, keeping him warm.

And alive.

"He probably wouldn't have made it without the dog," one of the rescue team members said. "He was lucky."

"That dog is a real protector," the sheriff added. "He wasn't going to let us touch your boy."

We felt blessed beyond belief. Our baby was back. No more resentment for me. Life and living were too precious. After that, when Bob and I would start picking at each other, we would only need to look at Robby playing with Blacky to realize whatever was bugging us just wasn't so important. Money was still an issue, but not worth fighting over.

Now we try to hash things out together. I've been working on staying on top of things like housework and not forgetting stuff. It's as though those hours when Robby was lost were our trial by fire.

Nightmares haunted me for a long time. I'd wake up shaking and Bob would hold me. He has strong comforting arms.

I told Marge about the nightmares one day. She said they'd go away eventually-and they did. Now I spend each day thanking God and reminding myself how blessed we are, especially as we amble through the woods and fields and Robby grabs my knee.

"Gotcha, Mommy."

I swing my son up into my arms and we rub noses, both of us giggling. Ah, what a gift, the laughter of a small child. I am so blessed. I can never say this often enough.

WHEN STUBBORN MEETS STUBBORN

"A pony!" I stared at the Shetland pony backing out of a trailer right in our yard. "For me?"

When I got excited I rubbed my clenched hands together and my face scrunched in a grin. I added jigging in place that night.

The man handed my dad the lead tied to the pony's halter. "Her name is Polly and she's pretty old, but she'll be a good first pony for your little girl." He smiled at me, standing by my mother. "You got a bridle or saddle?"

Daddy shook his head.

The man reached in the trailer and unhooked a bridle. "I'll pick this up sometime when I'm nearby. Oh, and Polly likes sugar cubes. I don't give her many, not good for her teeth, but she loves them."

"Thank you." Daddy and the man shook hands, then the man got in his truck and drove off. But I didn't watch that. All I could see was a pony who looked grizzled gray in the fading light. Dusk was creeping across the land, the cows were milked and chores done. A good time for a pony to arrive.

But when wasn't a good time for a pony?

I stood in front of her and just stared. My pony, name of Polly, was a dream of a lifetime. Even at five, it seemed I had wanted a pony forever. She nibbled at my fingers when I reached out to stroke her face, making me giggle.

Mom returned from the house and handed me a couple of sugar cubes. My dad liked to dunk a sugar cube in his coffee, just like his pa did.

"Give it to her on the flat of your hand," Daddy said. "She might be old but if she mistakes your fingers for a sugar cube...."

I nodded and did as told, giggling when her whiskers tickled my palm. "She likes it all right." I let her finish and held out the other.

"I'll bridle her up and then you can ride."

"Really?"

He looped the rope around her neck and unbuckled the halter. "She might try to take off on you so don't give her a chance." She took the bit without an argument, and he buckled the bridle in place. "You see how to do this so you can do it yourself next time."

I nodded, everything seemed to happen in slow motion. Polly swished her tail and stamped one front foot.

"Now, here you go. Hang on to the reins." Like most farm kids, I had ridden on our team of work horses, but I'd never ridden my own pony. Daddy picked me up and sat me on her back, reins in hand. He slapped her on the rump, and she took off, and I did too, only in the opposite direction, screaming all the while.

I still remember my mother screaming, "Don't kill her, Laurel."

I don't know how he caught her. I would always need a can of oats to bribe her with, but he caught her, set me up on her back again, and said, "Now hang on."

That was the best advice my father ever gave me. Hang on. And so began my years with Polly.

The dream had started some time before. When you are little, ten minutes can seem like forever. "Mommy, when we get to the farm, can I have a pony?"

"We shall see."

I studied her face. That was one of those puzzling lines along with "maybe". I have no idea when I started wanting a pony, but ponies and town living didn't mix. But now we were in Minnesota where my Daddy grew up before he went into the Navy. The war was over, and he was hoping to buy a dairy farm. A farm meant land and pasture for a pony. And lots of cows, which suited me fine, animal lover that I already was. We had a dog — a rat terrier — but a farm meant cows and horses and chickens, maybe pigs also. Surely we would have cats in the barn and in the house too.

The farm we now lived on had a big white barn with stanchions for the cows on both sides of the center aisle down the length and box stalls at either end. A silo guarded the barn and long machine shed. We also had a two-story house where the upstairs was divided into two bedrooms with slanted ceilings that made it seem cozier. My mom and dad had a bedroom downstairs. A black cast iron cook stove dominated the kitchen and provided heat for the house.

After our first rather surprising evening, Polly and I slowly became friends. She was an opinionated creature who did not like to be ordered around. She had lived many years and knew every trick in The Book of Shetland Pony Behaviors.

The Book

1. You do not come when called. You wait until you hear the oats rattling in the can. No oats in the can, you do not get caught.
2. You do not stand still the first time when your girl tries to get on your back. A handful of oats is the price.
3. If you do not feel the terrain is solid, no amount of leg banging and orders will persuade you. The best thing to do is whirl around and run for the barn.
4. When your girl wants to ride to her friend's house, you go as far as you feel like, then whirl and head for the barn. If the barn door is closed, you wheel and head for the gate. Stop as abruptly as possible.

5. If your rider happens to fall off, head for the barn.
6. If she yells at you, ignore her. She'll get over it.
7. Do not bite. Biting is bad pony manners.
8. After your girl has brushed you and sprayed you with water, go roll in the dusty place where all the horses roll.

....

I learned that even if I was in a bit of a hurry, I worked by her rules—or else. Polly did not like to be rushed. But I also learned how to work around her.

Take her not wanting to go away from the farm. I would mount by the lowest rail on the pole bar gate and cluck her into moving. I'd talk to her and pat her neck. The county road made a gentle ninety-degree turn on the other side of the farm fence in the corner of the section where the barn stood. On a good day we would trot out, round the corner, and start up to my friend Florence's house.

The road went down a short way and up a gentle hill to the next county road which bordered the west side of our farm. Turn left on that road, and Florence's farmhouse was a couple hundred feet away. Not a long ride by any means. I clutched the rope that worked as reins tied to Polly's halter and watched her ears. I'd keep talking to her, telling her how good she was being, and keep my bare legs ready for action. As soon as she tightened to turn, I bailed off, making sure to hang on to the reins. Then I dragged her the rest of the way to Florence's house. Sometimes I ended up in the dirt, but I kept getting better.

When it was time to go home, I would mount up, trot out to the road, and hang on while Polly went on a dead run clear to our barn. At our driveway she would hook a sharp left and plow to a stop at the barn. In those Bemidji summers, she would be dripping with sweat, and so would I. We girls only wore dresses then, and my long legs were strong from hanging on to Polly and itchy from riding a sweaty pony.

I remember my mother telling me years later that the mailman used to drive behind me, and once asked did they know how Polly and I did not look both ways before charging across the road? He also said I clung like a burr to that pony's back. Desperation is a good teacher. Determination, too.

Two summers later we moved to another farm out in Solway, Minnesota which might as well have been a world away for Florence and me. Since we were farming with milking cows, we didn't do a lot of visiting, mostly into Bemidji where my relatives lived. I'm not sure I ever saw Florence again, though we did write letters to each other, and I think it was in the next year that she died from cancer. When you are seven years old, that seems incomprehensible. But now as an adult, it still does.

I remember my cousins coming out to the farm, and my boy cousins planning to show me how to make Polly mind. Right. She wasn't very tall but oh my, she was strong. When she whirled and tore out, they did the same thing I did that first night we had her. I always told them what Daddy told me. Hang on.

When my cousins would come, we'd make ice cream in the crank freezer. We put a cake of ice in a gunny sack and slam the broad side of the axe against the sack until the ice was useable. Then we'd pour those ice chips into the crank machine. That was the best ice cream ever.

We had no electricity at that house, so we used kerosene lamps and lanterns and a big black wood cook stove. We milked the cows by hand and ran the milk through the separator, a machine of many cones that needed to be washed very carefully. That was one of my jobs during the summer.

Those summers Polly and I also became babysitters. While Mom and Dad worked the fields, hayed, and kept the farm going, I was in charge of my little brother and baby sister. They both loved to ride Polly, so I would put them on her back and lead her around. One time Polly stumbled and Karen fell off and got up with a perfect pony print on her cheek. I figured I was in for it then. But the bruise hardly showed, and my folks understood accidents.

During the winter, all our animals were kept in the barn and let out on nice days. Polly had her own stall in the barn. When I'd walk home from the bus stop, I'd stop at the house, leave my books, change my coat, and go out to the barn to see Polly. I rigged a harness for her so she could pull the sled with Don and Karen on it. You could conquer worlds with baling twine, including a harness — I braided twine for reins to go with that aging halter. I'd get oats in the can when I came into the barn, and when I shook it, Polly and the gray Percherons from Daddy's work team, Flossie and Myrtle, always nickered.

I came home from school one winter day to learn that Polly had died in her stall during the night. I understood that she was a very old pony but she'd not been sick or gave us any indications. Daddy figured she was forty-one when she died. But those last years of her life, she taught one little girl many lessons and provided hours of joy and companionship.

Besides the memories, more important were the life lessons. We all need to learn how to hang on to get through this life. Now when I speak before groups of all sizes, I tell people that was the best advice my father ever gave me: "Just hang on!"

Angel in Gold Fur

I wouldn't have to swim too far, she thought.

Huddled on a rock just above the spume line, Julia Ransome stared out over the gunmetal chop of Lake Ontario. Gray clouds, gray water, gray rock. But nothing compared to the gray inside. The wind blew off the water and right through her wool jacket, freezing the right breast that no longer was.

She and Miles had loved to sit on this very rock and watch the sunrise. But now he was enjoying eternal sunrises, and all she saw was gray.

So, how far? She wondered. *How long would it take? The water temperature is below forty-five degrees, so that means hypothermia in less than five minutes. Of course, the swimming would be good exercise if I could even lift my right arm far enough for a decent stroke. For that matter, I could just float on my back.*

So, now or tomorrow? What's there to wait for?

Her nose dripped in the cold; February in Toronto was beyond chill. Ice rimmed the beach. If only it were frozen enough so that she could just walkout until the ice gave way and dropped her in, deep enough to be beyond saving. With her luck, some do-gooder would come thrashing out to save her.

She'd have to do it at night.

Julia turned in surprise at the soft sound of a dog whimper. There, next to her rock, sat a golden retriever, head cocked, studying her with warm brown eyes. Gold amid gray. Quite a contrast.

"Beat it." She made shooing motions with her right hand that sent a shock up her shoulder. "Blast!" She winced. "The cold must be tightening it up." She flexed her shoulder and clasped her hands around her knees, refocusing her gaze back to the gray water.

The dog whined again.

Julia tried to return to her contemplation but she could no longer concentrate.

"What is it, dog? You lost or something?"

The golden tail feathered across the sand, and the dog raised one paw.

"Are you hurt?" Julia reached for the paw and then caught her breath. When would she get used to the pain? The doctor told her to exercise those muscles every day. He'd carefully led her through the whole program, but what was the use when one knew the days were few? She swung her legs off the rock and leaned forward enough so her reaching wouldn't bring on nausea. Even through her gloves she could feel the warmth of the dog's head as she stroked it. A lightening quick tongue kissed the end of her nose.

The right paw came up and rested on her knee.

Julia rubbed the golden ears and down the dog's neck until she found a collar. A dog bone shaped tag read Pepper. Turning it over, she found no numbers, neither phone nor identification.

"Pepper, eh?" The tail fanned the sand again and the dog scooched closer. "Well, you better be getting' on home, Pepper; it'll be dark in a few."

Julia stood and turning, looked up and then down the beach. The boardwalk ribboned along the shore, empty as if wearing signs of no trespassing. Even the sassy black squirrels with tufted ears had sworn off chattering and whisking their way up and down the oak trees in the park. A seagull mewled, its cry a dirge that matched her own. But at least the gull could shriek. Julia had tried that. It didn't help, so she'd sworn off shrieking and mewling.

She's do something about it instead. She took two strides toward the water lapping the sand and encountered a solid wall of dog, planted between her and the six inch surf.

"Get! Go home, you mangy mutt."

Pepper looked up at her with eyes full of... full of what? Warmth, love, pleading?

Julia backed up; the dog came with her.

"Look, Pepper, go home." She enunciated and donned her most dog-obey-me-now tone, the one that always worked with dogs or kids or whoever needed a firm word. But Pepper remained at her side, looking out over the wind-whipped water.

Julia looked up Willow Street, trying to figure which one of the houses might be missing a stubborn and opinionated golden retriever.

"You can't be a stray, too recent a brushing." She ran her hands down the dogs ribs, her right arm reminding her that she'd stretched again. "You haven't' missed many, if any, meals either. Did you get out of your yard?"

Pepper's head cocked slightly, and with pink tongue lolling, seemed to shrug.

"Well, you surely don't act too worried about it. Scoot now, get on home."

The dog continued to gaze across the lake.

Julia shivered. The blasted wind could turn one's bones to glacier ice. She stuck her fleece gloved hands into her pockets and glanced once more over the water. *Tomorrow*, she promised herself. *Tomorrow night.*

She started up the street, still feeling slightly off balance since her surgery.

Pepper paced her, step for step at her left knee.

Julia stopped halfway up to Queen Street. "Now, get this, dog. Go home." She motioned in an arc, giving the dog a choice of direction.

Pepper sat and looked at her, one eyebrow raised ever so slightly.

"Suit yourself." Julia strode on up the incline, ignoring the click of nails against the concrete sidewalk. At Queen Street, she waited for the light. Pepper sat. When the light changed, she stood and matched Julia's stride as she crossed the intersection.

"Someone sure must be missing a well-trained dog like you."

A kid yelled from the other side of the street. "Hey lady, don't ya know there's a leash law in town?"

"It's not my dog." The words sounded as stupid as she felt. Who'd believe it, a stray heeled like an obedience champion. Julia walked up on past the meat market to Cedar and turned left. So did Pepper.

"Well, you're going to have to go home; you can't come in, you know." She repeated herself at the top of the stairs to the front yard and again on the wide porch. Two Italianate urns still hoarded bits of the last snow, as did the north sides of houses and the shaded sidewalks where people had tossed snow from their walks. Dirty, gritty, gray slop now.

Pepper sat in front of the door, as if accustomed to waiting for a key to be found, inserted into the lock... and then what?

"No. You cannot come in. Your family must be frantic by now. Go on home." Julia brushed past the dog, slipping into the entry and shut the door behind her, even refusing to look out the square window shielded by the lace curtain. The storm door gave its final snick.

"There, and that's that." After unwinding her scarf, she placed it and gloves in a basket on the door then hung up her anorak. She closed the door to the closet, which was tucked neatly beneath the stairs, using just the right push to make the stubborn thing click. Miles had always intended to fix that old catch on the door.

After heating the water in the microwave, she let her tea bag steep while she flipped through the mail she'd stacked on the counter. The pink begonia that bloomed its heart out year round on the windowsill, hung in limp sorrow over the edges of the pot.

Throw it or water it? She fingered a translucent stem and leaf. At least it wasn't dried and brown. She poured a cup of tepid water on it, then carried her mug of steaming tea back into the living room. Dusk hung in the room. She curled up in the corner of the couch, not bothering to turn on a lamp to banish the shadows. The furnace kicked in with a click.

The Christmas tree still filled the front window, its needles collecting on the white and gold skirt. She hadn't turned on the tree's lights since the night Miles had his heart attack, but still couldn't marshal the energy to take the poor thing down.

"Why, Miles?" she pleaded. "Why did you have to leave like that?" She stared up at the ceiling. "God, if you love me like you say you do, then why-why did you take Miles?" She couldn't begin to count the times she'd asked those questions. Questions that had yet to be answered.

An angel wing, atop the withered tree, glinted from the flash of a passing car's lights. If Miles had become an angel, he'd not made an appearance yet.

But then again, angelhood was just another one of her unanswered questions.

Still it didn't matter, tomorrow she'd find out some of the answers for herself. She'd ask Miles face to face.

The streetlights painted tree shadows on her wall. Surely the dog had gone home by now. But on her way back to the kitchen, Julia peeked out the front door, just to see. There Pepper lay on the mat, curled in a tight circle, nose hidden in tail.

"Oh, for Pete's sake." Julia unlocked the dead bolt and swung open the door. "Why didn't you go home, you silly dog? Come in here before you freeze to death."

Pepper didn't need a second invitation. She scooted around the storm door and into the entry hall, tail wagging in approval. A happy sound like a loud purr rumbled from the dog's throat as she frisked around Julia's legs. Pepper gave a little yip before sniffing the entry rug, then glanced curiously at the walnut staircase before she came back to lean against Julia's legs, and the rumbling purr sounded again.

"So you talk, do you?" Julia leaned over to ruffle Pepper's ears, noticing the dog was a female. She stroked her golden head. "Poor girl. I suppose you're hungry too."

Pepper sat and lifted one paw, her well-shaped head at an angle that seemed to imply approval and all the while her tail swished back and forth across the floor.

"I don't have dog food, you know." Julia considered her cupboard and refrigerator, both singularly lacking in food in general, let alone anything suitable for a dog. She hadn't felt like shopping in weeks. She picked up a can. "Do you like chili?"

Pepper smiled her total agreement.

Julia opened the can and poured the chili into a large bowl before setting it in the microwave. "Might taste better if I nuke it a little."

Pepper just sat nearby watching every move.

When Julia set the warm bowl on the floor, Pepper glanced at it and then back to Julia, but made not a move. "Okay, girl, it's yours. Have at it."

Pepper ate daintily, at a steady pace, and licked every trace from the bowl. Then she sat and wagged her tail.

"You need a drink?" Julia filled the bowl with water and set it back down. Once again, when invited, Pepper lapped until satisfied.

The evening stretched ahead of her, empty like all the rest since her son, Darren, and his wife, Cindy, had left after the funeral. They'd both needed to get back to their jobs. She understood how their lives on the West Coast kept them too busy to visit very often. And while her son loved her and promised to keep in touch, the phone calls petered out after a few weeks. Before, the distance hadn't mattered so much. Now even the phone seemed too heavy to lift.

"You can sleep in the basement tonight and tomorrow we find your owner, okay?" Julia led the way to the basement, taking an old coat off the hook on her way down the stairs. "This should make you a good bed, the washroom is plenty warm."

She set another bowl of water down on the floor, arranged the coat and pointed to the makeshift bed. "There you go." Pepper sniffed the coat, then sat in the middle. Julia ruffled the dog's ears and stroked her head, earning a wrist kiss for her efforts. "Ah, you are a sweet dog, aren't you?" Pepper rumbled and raised one ear, her tail wagging all the while.

Julia closed the door, shutting off the lights as she went. She adjusted the heat for the night and made her way upstairs. On many nights the stairs seemed too much of a challenge and she'd simply doze off on the couch and then awaken half frozen.

She stared around her disheveled bedroom. She should straighten things up here if tomorrow was really the day. Shame to let Darren come in to such a mess. Should she write a note? That way they'd know what happened and not think it a homicide. Surely, she should set her affairs in order.

Instead, she pulled on her fleecy, footed pajamas. Nights had been so desperately cold without Miles. Lying next to him had been like sleeping with a cozy bed warmer-one with arms and a beating heart.

She clicked on the remote to the TV, Flicking through channels like a man. Her thumb coordination on the remote had improved in the last weeks, but that was about the only part of her body that seemed to work these days. As usual, nothing caught her interest. She glanced over at the Bible on her nightstand. At first she'd searched for comfort within its pages but the words seemed as flat and lifeless as the two dimensional bodies moving across the television screen.

Only the heaving icy lake offered comfort. *Tomorrow night for sure.*

She woke sometime later to a dog's tongue licking away her tears.

"What?" she cried. "Pepper, how'd you get up here?" That familiar purring sound and the cold nose where her only answers as the dog eased down besides her, resting her head on Julia's left shoulder. "You should get down," warned Julia. But the warm body simply snuggled closer. Julia scratched the dog's ears and stroked her silken head. Pepper sighed.

Julia did too. But instead of getting up and pacing the floor, as had become her habit when waking in the middle of the night, she remained in bed, continuing to pet the dog until she fell back asleep. She didn't wake until the chime of the doorbell sent Pepper bounding from the bed and down the stairs. Julia struggled into her robe. Getting her right arm into the sleeve of this loose fitting garment without pain was yet to be accomplished.

The bell chimed again.

"All right, all right," she called. "I'm coming." The clock showed nine. Must be the mailman. She belted her robe as she descended the stairs, careful not to let the back of her slippers catch on the risers. A tumble down the stairs might mess up her plans.

Pepper stood at attention, her nose to the door, tail wagging cautiously. She looked over her shoulder as if to ask, are you coming?

"Pepper, sit."

Pepper obeyed.

Julia brushed her hair back with her left hand, then reached for the doorknob with her right. The pain of the movement made her whimper. Pepper stood at attention, her gaze drilling the door with a protective glance in Julia's direction.

"No, it's okay girl. Sit." The dog had gone on guard for her, but now sat obediently. Julia opened the door and reached for the slender package. "Thanks."

"Hope you're feeling better," the mail carrier said.

"I'm fine thank you," she replied, closing the door with a snap. *What a liar I've become! But what else can I say? Thank you very much, I'm so fine that I plan to walk across Lake Ontario today-underwater.*

Pepper sniffed the mail and turned through the arch into the living room, again looking over her shoulder, as if expecting Julia to follow.

"No," Julia answered in a matter-of-fact tone. "I'm not sitting down to read the mail today. You see, I don't read the mail anymore. Just like I don't answer the telephone." The stack on the coffee table seemed obvious proof of that.

If anyone heard me justifying myself to a dog…

She dumped the mail on the growing pile and walked through the opened French doors into the dining room and then onto the kitchen. She could write her good-bye letter in the dust on the ancient pine table- or any other flat surface in her house for that matter. Shae stared at the table. Miles should be sitting there, with his back to the sunshine that often streamed in that window. He loved the warm sunlight on his shoulders, his steaming cup of coffee, his morning paper.

She'd discontinued taking the paper. The sun had discontinued itself.

Pepper stood before the sink, tail wagging, and another glance over the shoulder.

"You hungry?" The tail wagged faster. "Chili again?" More wagging. The tail brushed softly against her dark fleece robe, leaving long golden hairs behind. "How about going outside while I fix your breakfast?"

The rumble purr again. Assent perhaps? Pepper followed her down the four steps to the back door and slipped out almost before Julia had it open. Within minutes the dog whined at the door until Julia opened it, and then headed directly right for the bowl of chili, lapping it up until the bowl shined. "Today we find your owner," said Julia as she placed the bowl in the sink.

"I'll start with the phone," she announced as she sat down and picked up the phone directory, grimacing at the weight. Pepper rested her chin on Julia's knee as she first dialed the Humane Society, then the local veterinarians, and finally the pet stores to see if there had been any notice of a lost dog. But no one knew anything about a missing golden retrieved who answered to the name Pepper. Julia's tea grew cold, and Pepper stretched out for a snooze, her muzzle now nestled on Julia's feet.

After a bit, Julia's stomach grumbled, the first time she'd noticed hunger since-when? She shrugged. Strange. Not that she'd sworn off eating altogether, but nothing seemed to suit her, and she never actually felt hungry. Perhaps heating the chili had triggered her hunger response.

Unless she wanted the last can of chili, the cupboard only yielded stale water crackers and a jar of peanut butter. Her stomach rumbled again. She could get dressed and go out to get something. The very thought made her ravenous. She had to eat-now! Quickly crisping the crackers in the microwave, she spread the peanut butter, nibbling from one while her tea water heated. Then she took the whole plateful and returned to the living room wondering whom else she could call to discover the owners of this dog? One by one, she ate the crackers, slipping bits to the dog who watched every bite but never begged once.

"Someone *must* be missing you, girl! You surely didn't fall out of the sky, did you?" She leaned over and cupped the dog's face in both her hands, touching her forehead to the animal's. "Ah, you are so beautiful and I-and I-" She stopped herself, wondering what she must do. *I can't care for this dog-why, I can't even care for myself! I don't know how to find her home and she can't stay here-all alone. But how can I abandon her either?*

Her cheek felt a quick lick, and she realized that tears she hadn't even noticed were being swiped by a warm tongue. Sitting upright, she wiped the back of her hand under her eyes. "Thanks, Pepper, but that wasn't exactly what I had in mind." *How come since this dog arrived, I've been crying all over the place again?*

She leaned back into the soft cushions of the couch, one hand still absently caressing Pepper's head. *Ah God, this hurts so bad. I'm ripped in half, and half a body can't live.*

"I don't want to go on like this!"

Pepper put both paws on her knees and stared right up into her face.

"Get down, girl. Can't you see..." But Pepper whined and leaned forward, her dark eyes so full of love that her tears started all over again. This time she wrapped both arms around Pepper's neck and sobbed into the gold fur. Pepper made her way onto the couch and snuggled right into Julia's lap, leaning, it seemed, directly into her grief.

Sometime later Julia awoke, her eyes burning, but her body actually warm for a change. The golden dog was still stretched out on her half way, her soft golden fur like an afghan. *Warm,* how blessed warm felt. She gently nudged the dog. "I think we better get you some dog food, eh, girl? Do you like to ride in the car? Who knows, maybe we'll even find your owner." Julia's brow creased. "And then, well, I'll just give them your food, and we'll send you on home."

But they didn't see an owner or anyone looking for a lost canine companion, and Pepper didn't show the slightest interest in any of the houses they passed as they cruised up and down the streets on both sides of Queen. Besides groceries and dog food, a leash, dog brush, and doggie treats filled the paper bags.

"After all," Julia explained to her new friend, "dogs must be kept on a leash in our town."

By late afternoon, no one had retuned her calls with any information regarding the dog or owner. So she snapped the leash onto Pepper's collar and off they went. Gray clouds ghosted the treetops as they walked up the hill, away from the waterfront. No sense going to the lake since she couldn't do what she planned anyway.

In the park, Pepper found a stick. Removing the leash, Julia took the stick and threw it. No overhand throw like she might have done just months ago. Now she tossed carefully, swinging underhand from the elbow. But her ravaged muscles screamed just the same. Despite the cold, beads of sweat popped out on her forehead. Pepper, tail spinning in delight, retrieved the stick and laid it at Julia's feet.

"You could just hand it to me, you know." But Julia forced herself to bend down anyway. To her surprise, stretching her back and legs felt surprisingly good. She threw the stick again-and yet again, wondering if stick throwing was on the list of acceptable exercises for postradical-mastectomy patients? Just the same, she suspected anything she did at this stage would make her doctor cheer.

Back at the house, she put her outer clothing away, then turned in alarm at the sound of Pepper whimpering. Following the sound, she found the dog, belly to the floor and nose pressed against the edge of the sofa.

"What is it, girl?"

Pepper looked over her shoulder then stuck her muzzle beneath the narrow space under the couch next to the carved wooden foot.

"What?"

Another whimper.

Julia slowly got down on her hands and knees, flinching at the effort. She tried to crouch low enough to see what Pepper saw, and the pain increased. Something once so simple now seemed utterly impossible! But Pepper whimpered again, compelling Julia to roll to her seat then onto her back, and finally she rolled over to her stomach. With her cheek against the hardwood floor she spied enough dust bunnies to fill a forest. And way back in the corner sat a bright, yellow tennis ball.

"Pepper, I can't possibly reach that." The dog whined pitifully, tail feathering, a pleading expression in her dark brown eyes.

Julia rolled back to her seat, then pulled her knees into a crouching position and slowly rose up, barely using her arms. Leading with her chin put strain on her other muscles but somehow she made it to her feet. She fetched the broom from the backstairs landing and returned to the couch where Pepper waited expectantly. This time she dropped to her knees and swept the broom back and forth until the tennis ball finally rolled free. Pepper snatched it up and tossed the yellow object in the air. Suddenly Julia recalled how much Miles had loved tennis. Her eyes burned, but the tears stayed at bay.

"So, now I am supposed to throw that for you, eh? Well, you'll just have to wait a moment." Then she swung the broom back and forth beneath the sofa evicting the errant bunnies along with hundreds of fallen fir needles. She swept everything into a neat pile, and went to retrieve a dustpan, but met another quandary. "Stupid useless arm." She chided herself. Pepper looked at her, head cocked, panting slightly.

If you'd just done what the doctor ordered…

"I know, I know." She bent from the waist, filling the dustpan and straightening with a loud groan.

Pepper met her in the kitchen, ball in mouth. Julia tossed it down the hall toward the front door, and Pepper raced after it, skidding on the area rug next to the door. Julia felt the strange sensation of a laugh gurgling in her throat. Pepper tossed the ball in the air and caught it in her mouth, tail spinning joyfully. Again and again she brought the ball to Julia, eager for the game to continue. Julia tossed the ball down the stairs, under the dining room table, even bounced it off the wall and watched the dog leap into the air to catch it. Finally, Julia cried, "That's all," and hid the ball in her hands behind her back.

Later in the evening, she showed the dog the makeshift bed in the laundry room once again. "Now, Pepper, she warned. "Dogs sleep down here, do you understand?" Pepper cocked her head, tongue lolling and eyes dancing. Julia glanced at the door, wondering how the dog managed to escape the previous night. *I must not have shut it securely, that's all.*

Taking time to prepare for bed, she brushed her teeth, washed her face, and even combed her hair, stopping just short of spritzing herself with the fragrance Joy. She stared at the bottle in her hand, remembering how this had been her nightly ritual through the many years with Miles. He loved the aroma of Joy. He loved her breasts. But when he heard the doctor say "one must go," he'd simply replied the Julia was a whole lot more than a pair of breasts.

Ah, Miles, you worried about my cancer and all the while your heart was ticking the final countdown. Once again, tears sprang to her eyes, rolling down her cheeks before she could stop them. Her vision blurred with tears as she slipped into her footed pajamas.

"Ah, Father in heaven, I *hate* this. Let me loose, please, free me." Hearing a sound behind her, she turned in alarm to see the golden dog gracefully leaping into bed.

"How'd you get out?" But Pepper simply waited for Julia to join her. Julia shook her head and climbed into bed. The dog snuggled close, her fur absorbing Julia's tears as she drifted off to sleep, her fingers entwining on the soft furry coat.

Once again, Pepper kept her warm throughout the night. And like a living alarm clock, she woke her in the morning for a mercy run out the back door.

Together they walked and played … and Julia even laughed.

And a week later, fresh snow blanketed the city. Pepper put her nose to the ground and plowed a rut clear across the backyard, then she rolled in it, tongue pink and legs kicking. Julia tossed her a snowball and Pepper caught in on the fly, then dropped it and gave her a look that clearly said, *not fair.* Julia laughed.

That evening, Julia stood, hand on her hips, studying her forlorn Christmas tree still standing in the living room. It was so pitiful it could even make Charlie Brown's tree look glamorous. "First thing tomorrow, Pepper-you want to help me take this thing down?"

Pepper rumbled in agreement, then nudged Julia's knee, looking longingly upstairs.

"Are you ready for bed already?"

Tail wagging, Pepper started up.

"All right." Together they mounted the risers.

The next morning, Julia stood at the sink staring out the window without really looking until a new bloom on her begonia caught her attention. "Hey, Pepper, this plant didn't die after all." Pepper looked at the plant then back to Julia, smiling as if she understood.

"Come on, girl, let's take a walk." Julia got out the leash and Pepper grabbed the end, headed for the front door while Julia put on her outerwear. Leash in place, they paced down the hill this time, instead of up toward the park. Theirs were the first tracks in the new snow that had fallen during the night.

Sunlight kissed the tips of the small swells on a lake so blue it almost made Julia's eyes ache. Cotton puff clouds swabbed the sky clean, and diamond-decked ice lace skirted the rocks in the water.

Julia brushed the top hat of snow off her favorite rock and perched to look over the water. Pepper leaped up and sat by her side.

"Beautiful, eh, Pepper?" Julia turned to see an empty rock. Pepper was gone.

A white-robed figure leaned over to ruffle the ears of the golden dog. "Been on another mission, eh, Pepper?"

When Heigh Ho Silver Came to Our House

"We got a horse!"

I announced it to all the kids in our neighborhood, if you could call our small farms along Frontier Road, a neighborhood. I started announcing when I got on the school bus that Monday morning and by the time we got off the bus that afternoon, everyone was planning on coming to see Silver. Someone finally had a horse.

I had dreamed of another horse of my own ever since my pony, Polly, died the last winter we lived in Minnesota. We moved to Washington State that summer when I was ten, but to town. Bremerton became our new home, but several years later, my Dad and Mom got their dream to buy another farm and I was that much closer to my "someday" horse.

Ecstatic does not begin to cover my joy and jumping-up-and-down delight when a white horse backed out of the trailer and on to our driveway. His name was Silver. While he didn't have the class of the Silver on Lone Ranger, he was mine—or rather he belonged to all three of us kids.

But I was the horse lover.

We rode him around the pasture that afternoon, bridle, but no saddle, and I led him when my little sister Karen rode. We all learned how to stay on, guide him with the reins, he was trained western, and bask in the thrill of having a horse again.

He seemed friendly, enjoying the attention, as I brushed him, combed out his tail, checked hooves, kissed his nose, and inhaled the oh so wonderful fragrance of horse. How I had missed that. While he was all white, his skin was dark in places, white in others and pink around his muzzle with dark freckles. From the way he arched his neck and carried his head and tail, he looked to be part Arab, and who knew what else. Silver enjoyed chunks of carrot, oats and crunched a peppermint hard candy. Then spread his lips wide and shook his head, making me laugh. I laughed a lot that day, sheer joy. I had a horse again. Wait until my friends met Silver. I knew for certain, he would become my best friend and we'd have many adventures, as we lived near miles of roads left over from logging the miles of woods.

On our much-missed farm in Minnesota, we'd had a Percheron team, along with Polly, so we were used to caring for feet, feeding and loving horses. Or at least I was, the other two were pretty small when we left the farm. When we let Silver out in the pasture that afternoon, I leaned on the gate, watching him drop to his knees, and roll, feet kicking in the air. He got up, shook himself, dust flying, and ambled off, nibbling the ankle deep grass and acquainting himself with his new territory.

Fast forward to Monday. I could hardly sit still all day. A horse, I had a horse at home. I drew horses on my tablet, wrote Silver ten different ways, and got caught passing a note to my best friend.

The teacher read it aloud. "You're coming, aren't you?" He stared at me. "Are you inviting all of us then? And to what may I ask are we coming."

Death by embarrassment was a real fear for this one. Or a wish at that point.

I spoke to my desk. "To see my new horse."

He heaved a long suffering sigh. "You realize there are a lot of blackboards that need washing and erasers cleaned?"

Eyes glued shut, I pleaded silently, please don't make me stay after school. Please don't. I'll do the chores for a week if you just let me go home today. The walk home was a long mile and no one was there to come pick me up. Besides, I knew that if someone were there, they would not come pick me up for a reason such as this. You paid your penalties yourself. Besides, my dad would say, "the walk will give you plenty of time to think about not passing notes again."

Back to the classroom. "Since this is your first offense, you are excused but should I catch you passing notes again, the penalty will be double."

"Yes, sir, thank you, sir." Relief melted me into the seat.

School finally let out. About ten kids from ages six (my sister Karen) to my twelve promised they'd be at our house as soon as they could get there. I'd never changed clothes so fast. I grabbed something to eat and the three of us Clauson kids headed for the pasture. Our dad worked at his brother's paving company and our mother was back to nursing, this time at the navel hospital in Bremerton. She'd worked only on the farm while we lived in Minnesota so it was a culture shock for us kids when she went back to work full time. This farm we'd bought was not crops and milk cows like in the Midwest, this was a chicken ranch and a thousand laying hens take a lot of work.

I got out a can with enough oats in the bottom to rattle well and we went to the fence, me dreaming of my horse trotting up to the fence when I whistled but reminding myself that Silver had to learn my whistle. As the other kids arrived, I practiced whistling and shaking the oats in the coffee can. Come on Silver, at least raise your head and notice us. We opened the gate and all of us trooped through. My dad had warned me to make sure I closed the gate so I did so, and made sure the wire loop was over the post.

Our six acres of pastures were divided by several fences and Silver had chosen to graze in the largest one. We walked on out to where he grazed, watching our approach with head held high. I rattled the oats, calling "come on Silver, meet all our friends."

He just stood there, tail swishing the flies, ears flicking back and forth.

He was not a big horse, about 14.5 hands, which would make it easier to mount him. I had tried grabbing a piece of mane and swinging aboard the day before, but real riders made it look a lot easier than it was. I did manage to mount however with a running leap, belly flat against his backbone. He'd not tried to get away, although someone was holding him at the time—-just in case.

As we drew closer, I shook the can more enticingly and called him in my most winsome tone. He watched face on.

"Easy, fellah, come on now, let's meet your new friends."

We were about ten feet away, all giggly and excited when that horse pinned his ears flat to his head, bared his teeth and charged! It was every kid for himself. You have never seen ten kids run for the fence and get through or roll under three strands of barb wire in so little time. Expecting that horse to be right on our heels, we looked back to see him in about the same spot placidly grazing. The spilled can of oats had already disappeared.

We got a mean horse. How could he act like this? He'd been so good the day before? For some odd reason no one wanted to go with me to try again, not that I wanted to either but I had to save face, somehow.

I checked everyone over. No horse bites, only two barbwire scratches and a couple of ripped shirt from that same barb wire. I never knew we could all get through a fence so fast.

Needless to say, no one rode. No one petted the horse. We now had a pasture ornament, good for keeping the pasture grazed.

Over the next few months, I tried every way to catch that horse but the time I tried to brave his charge out, when he got close enough, he spun and lifted his back hooves like he was going to kick me clear over the barn. Had I known how to throw a lasso, I would have caught him with that. He ate hay with the cows and enjoyed his life of leisure through the months until our first snow. Quickly, his hooves packed with snow and he was forced to hobble around.

I knew I had to help him. But how? My brother Don and I drove him into a smaller pen, oat can in hand and halter with rope over my arm, I walked up to him. He laid back his ears, I kept talking to him. He stumbled spinning to kick and I laid a hand on his rump, first time since we got him. His ears went forward and he turned his head to look at me over his shoulder. Keeping one hand on his back, I made my way to his neck, slid the rope around his neck and buckled the halter in place, muttering all the while. Don handed me the can of oats. I fed Silver a handful and walked him over to tie him at the board fence.

All I had to do was put a hand on him. Eventually we learned that even twine was enough rope for him to figure he was caught. From then on, we used a long twine to box him into a corner, get a hand on him and then he gave up. He never, ever kicked or bit any of us.

I cleaned the ice out of his hooves, the snow melted and through the winter months, when weather permitted I rode him all around our pastures, then out on the country roads and on to the miles of logging roads.

But my training by Silver was just beginning. Step one: catch me. Step two: understand that I will not take you where it is not safe to go; muddy, swampy areas, low hanging branches, deep brush, and near other animals who might be dangerous. He taught me about changing leads, playing broom and basketball polo, and how to make him rear, just like the real Heigh Ho Silver. Through the years I learned to trust him with non riders. I watched him shift to the side when a small child was on his back and sliding. He always walked carefully, more like a mule than many horses. I learned to trim his feet, feed him cigarettes for worming and slap a combination of molasses and turpentine on his tongue when he got wheezy from dusty hay in the winter. While these were old fashioned treatments told me by an old horseman, they worked.

We learned that if you squeezed his flanks with your heels he would buck. If someone who thought they were hotshot riders got on him, they got a real ride, sometimes hard on their pride. He was downright crafty with people who thought they knew more than they did. And of course, we—er—I might have suggested they squeeze his flanks to make him pick up his feet better.

We didn't really know his history but the first time I rode him in a community parade, when the band began to play, Silver strutted to the music. When the band in marching formation, turned and marched the other way, so did we. Later we learned somehow that he'd been owned by a military officer at one time who had indeed ridden him in parades.

How often I wished that horse could talk and tell me of all his adventures. Through "Old" Silver we called him, I not only learned horse tending and riding skills but persistence, observation and trust. I guess God's been teaching me to trust all my life, to depend on someone else's wisdom, even that of a white horse. I learned a foreign language, ie: equine ear speak, along with the economics of owning animals since I had to pay for shoeing, (which was why I learned to shoe him myself) vet calls, my saddle, tack and any other sundry expenses.

I eventually bought a Saddle-bred/Morgan mare named Kit and Silver kept on training my brother and sister, cousins, friends and all those we brought his way. After I left home for college and Don and Karen weren't riding, our folks gave Silver to a family down the road with small children so he could keep on training new kids. And to think, the greatest gift of all was the guts to ignore his buffaloing and put a hand on his rump. The real lesson being learning to look beyond body language, especially masks, to see the heart. Only looking back can I see the real lessons that I learned from that old white horse. He was silver indeed, one of those dreams come true that God used in far more ways than I could ever dream—or desire.

CHEWEY

We fell in love with Bassets years ago when our neighbor in Vancouver, WA took in a rescue dog. Missy, the Basset, was shy and obviously had been abused. As she came out of the trauma, she adopted us, and took charge of patrolling our place along with her own. Every day she made the rounds, came in for her loves and a treat and kept on. As time went on, when her mom and dad traveled she stayed with us, but every day, she checked out both houses. Leaving her when we moved she was one of the goodbyes hard on my heart.

When we moved from Washington state to California we lived in apartments for a couple of years, then rented a house. One of my writing students kept saying, "get a Basset, get a Basset, the only thing they wear out in one spot on the carpet where they sleep all the time." So one day we found a Basset rescue, and Woofer came to live with us. He and our cockatiel, Bidley, moved with us to our new house in Tehachapi, California.

Years are harder on dogs than people and eventually he developed some heart problems, handled by medication. On one of our trips for my writing business, the kennel where Woofer stayed when we were gone, called and said he was failing, it was time. Coming home to no dog took all the joy out of being home again, especially when husband Wayne said, "No more dogs."

That was in October and I left him alone until about March when I started the campaign. I began talking dog again—and again. I said things like "I think I'll find a yellow lab when I have a dog again" or "I wonder if Golden Retrivers come as short haired dogs." We had taken care of our two Golden granddogs for nine months and they were absolutely heart stealers. Goldens are pure love wrapped up in gold fur. Lots of gold fur that sheds and sheds. I threatened to spin the fur and knit a sweater until a friend said "think what wet dog smells like."

My campaign continued. "Did you see the ad for that lab cross in the paper. She needs a home, says she eight years old. I think I want an older dog this time, they are harder to place in rescue."

I progressed to, "When we get our next dog, spring is a good time."

One day he said. "I want another Basset."

So the search began. I learned that there was a Basset Rescue in Acton, California, about an hour and a half from our house. I called. They were only open to viewing on the weekends. I called for an appointment. They were not open the next weekend. I went back to the calendar. No time for three weeks. Would we ever get a dog?

I wanted a dog. Our house needed a dog. Wayne needed a dog whether he knew it or not.

Finally the day came. We invited our neighbors to go with us, we'd stop for lunch and go see the Bassets. Dawn who ran the rescue had given us directions both how to get there and how to navigate the double gate. We finally found it and parked where she had told us. The kennel was up a bit of a rise, it was a beautiful day and we stretched and laughed and headed for the gates.

The world broke loose in Basset bays. More Bassets than I had ever seen came aroohing down to the gate. We now understood the value of a double gate with a greeting room in between as some slipped past the quick closure we tried. Once into the main yard, I thought sure I had died and gone to heaven. We got the royal greeting, patted some and headed up the hill where Dawn stood laughing at our reactions.

Bassets of every age, color, markings and voice milled around us then went off nose to the ground to check out the daily news. Dawn gave us the grand tour and some history and we ended up in the general purpose room full of dog beds, old sofas, blankets and Bassets. These were all the sociable critters, there were others in runs down the long kennel who were not ready for adoption yet.

Dawn and I chatted more about what we felt we needed or were looking for and she told us she had thought about what dog might work for us. She introduced us to about eight dogs, she had somewhere between seventy-five and a hundred, and I asked a million questions. I walked them, and petted them and rubbed bellies and fell in love with all of them. One male, I was leaning toward a female, the largest dog went and sat between Wayne's feet. His name was Chewey and he waited. I got bitten by the little female I was looking at, as I moved too quickly and she had been abused, so I told her sorry, she would not be going home with us.

Our neighbors were getting a bit impatient. Wayne was giving me the rolling eye look and I reminded him of our agreement, *I* got to make the choice *this* time. I rubbed bellies and asked questions and tried to decide. Surely I would find just the perfect dog in this many. I glanced over. Chewey hadn't moved. Wayne was not petting him even.

A few more minutes and Wayne said, "I think we have been chosen." And pointed to Chewey.

Dawn grinned from ear to ear. "Excellent choice."

They didn't know much about him, other than they had his papers, he had been owner surrendered and the first thing they did was neuter him. She said he was socialized, and five years old.

We paid our required amount and loaded all of us in the van. Our neighbors kept petting him and he lay between the seats without a murmur. He traveled well. He ate well, he walked well, Chewey took over.

I said, "no dog on beds or sofa. The dog sleeps on the floor." Uh huh. That lasted about ten hours—-maybe. I said, "do not feed the dog from the table." Two meals and Chewey waited intently until Dad slipped him the last bite of his toast. At least he did not grab or snap at the treat. He ate anything, vacuumed any spilled crumbs and cleaned up the kitchen floor when I decorated it with spaghetti sauce.

Several days into this adventure, I found a loaf of bread, or rather a partial loaf of bread on the floor. We did not have a cat, no kids, how did the bread end up on the floor? Chewey cleaned up the crumbs and life continued. He slept in the middle of the bed or diagonally if possible. He snored.

Two thawing hamburger patties disappeared off the counter. We have a tall counter. What had happened? Surely not? I looked down at the dog grinning at my feet, the innocent dog smiling up at me.

A few days later we caught him in the act. Chewey was a counter cruiser, an experienced counter cruiser. There was no breaking him, we jerked on his leash, we said no, we sprayed him with water—-we learned to *never* leave anything on the counter. Never! We learned things needed to be pushed to the middle of the island. We warned everyone who came to our house because he not only cleaned off counters but coffee tables and tv trays were an opportunity not to be missed.

Trainers said, "Catch him in the act and firmly tell him no." Right.

We put up a gate finally but what a hassle that could be. We gave up. After all, he had trained us to clear off the counters, not a bad idea. When food needed to be thawed, I put it in the sink.

One day I put a whole chicken to thaw in the sink. I found it in the middle of the living room floor, but not all of it. No matter what he ate, he never got sick, not even from the chocolate he found under the Christmas tree.

But Chewey was not my dog, he was Dad's dog. He had chosen Dad and that was just the way it was. As a friend said, "Wayne is DAD, you are Not Dad."

Chewey went everywhere with Dad, even to riding in the bus Wayne was converting into a motor home. When Chewey went down in the rear, Wayne spent two months in the dining room, with Chewey in a small pen, red roofing paper and newspapers on the floor. Wayne kept watch, working with his buddy as slowly, thanks to coaching from the people on the Daily Drool, an online Basset group, Dawn of Daphneyland where we got him, Dr. Frang who administered acupuncture and supervised the meds and the prayers of many, our dog was walking again. He no longer slept on the bed or the sofa but with help, he could climb up in the bus and keep on traveling with us for two more years.

He was twelve when what I thought was an abscessed tooth was in reality cancer. Surgery was not an option since half the lower jaw would be removed and chemo had not proved effective with this kind of cancer. Chewey kept on going. The vet said, "he will tell you when it is time." Chewey kept on going. He knew his mission was to take care of Wayne and he held on. One day I had to say, "Wayne, we can't let him suffer like this." He never told us when the time came, some dogs are like that. So sometimes we have to make that heart rending decision. His love for Dad kept him going. We really called him Sir Chewey of de Mountains. He was indeed, king of the mountains and king of our hearts. Maybe someday I'll have a dog.

Dogs Know

Written for Judy Auger by Lauraine Snelling

I have always known that dogs are smart, but I did not know how much dogs know until I met Buffy. I didn't plan for her to come into my life, in fact, our lives. My husband Gery, was very ill, his body shutting down bit by bit. For the last years, he had said, "No dogs," because he was afraid of tripping over one. It seemed wise so I agreed, with the thought that I would probably never have another dog. Somehow that didn't seem important at the moment. Taking care of Gery was. After years of diabetes and complications, his body was shutting down.

And then Buffy showed up. One day we were visiting our son Jon and his family at their home in Bakersfield. A few days earlier they'd had an unexpected visitor, a terrified scruffy little dog who had been chased into their yard by a bigger dog. They had dutifully searched for the owners but no one had responded

When we came, Jon looked at us both, and said, "Mom, Dad, I think this dog is supposed to be yours." I looked at Gery, fully expecting to see him shaking his head and saying, "No," with his lovely French accent. But he was very quiet. He looked at me, and he looked at Jon, and he said, "Yes. We'll take this little dog."

You can guess that I about fell off my chair, but Buffy came home with us. The name Scruffy fit her but we decided on Buffy to fit in with Jon's dogs who all started with the letter B.

She was scruffy, but after a bath and grooming we realized she's a fluffy probably terrier mix with unbounded energy and a lightening quick tongue that licked anyone within licking distance. We learned she looked best when she was about half cut so you could see her lovely brown spots and one little black dot all on a white body with fluffy, fluffy hair. She had a long tail that feathered and wagged and wagged, and wagged.

Buffy grew into her legs and body in the months after she came to live with us and as she grew we learned she was fast. She could zip around faster than any dog that I have seen, so maybe there was some greyhound in her. I have no idea. She had a little mustache and a bit of an overbite and dark, warm, warm, brown eyes that seemed to say, "Hey, I'm yours, and I am de-lighted!" From the first moment on, she glued herself to Gery.

Now, in the past, dogs had pretty much been mine because I took care of them. But Gery needed her, and that was when I began to understand how much dogs know. She never left his side, and he had his hand on her all the time. That was so unlike Gery. I was surprised because Buffy was energy in motion until she was with Gery, sitting in his lap, lying in his lap, sleeping in his lap, sleeping beside him, with him; always loving him with those big brown eyes. And lightening tongue.

Only months passed as Gery steadily weakened. Hospice came in to help us but he didn't live much longer. Buffy stayed right beside him until the men carried his body out. She searched the house for him but attached herself to me. She looked at me with those compassionate eyes, and I felt like she said, "Okay, Mom. We're in this together. It's okay. It's going to be okay." I knew it would be because Gery was so ready to go home. Now my life with Buffy had begun, because she knew that I was the needy one.

So, as my life as a widow begins, the dance of grief has begun. One step forward, sometimes two back. It's a slow dance but it's easier with a dog.

I've learned that Buffy loves everyone but she takes care of me. She makes sure I get enough exercise so we walk a lot. She makes sure that I bend over because she isn't quite all the way housebroken yet, or at least she wasn't until lately. She makes sure that I eat because she makes sure that she eats. It's very easy when you're a widow and trying to learn to live all over again to forget to cook, or even eat. She makes sure that I get rest. I'm a restless sleeper, but I know that she knows that I should be lying still because she can sleep better when I'm lying still. So, I do, and then, amazingly, I sleep. She reminds me to laugh as she zips around our house, or a friend's house, down the halls, over the furniture, under the table around me and repeat. Perhaps even again. Laughter is like applause to her. She skids to a stop in front of me and preens her pride.

And now, amazingly, the first and they say, the hardest, year has passed. We have been through all the holidays, the family special days and the horrendous paper work required even when the affairs were all in order. Glitches happen. Tears still attack, trying to drown me at times but I have learned, mostly from others who have lost a loved one, that this is a normal part of the dance. Buffy dries my tears and needs me like I need her. She goes most everywhere with me, my constant companion; a gift I had no idea how much I would need. As I said, dogs know.

Wolf to the Rescue

Silence from in the sod house. Ingeborg Bjorklund bent to remove the bars across the doorway to keep her young son Andrew safe and stepped inside. Blinking to adjust her eyes to the dimness, she crossed to the stove and lifted the lids to check the firebox. Out.

"Thorliff, could you please bring in some wood?"

"Ja, we will."

Ingeborg crossed the room and stopped by the bed. No little body mounded the covers. The bed was empty.

"Andrew, Andrew, where are you?" Ingeborg spun around, frantically searching each nook and cranny. "If you are hiding, come on out, I have bread and sugar for you." But Andrew was not in the soddy.

"Thorliff, go call for Andrew, will you? He must have climbed over the bars. You and Baptiste search the barn." Thoughts of what could happen to a little one who climbed into the boar's pen tore through her mind. Or what if he fell in the well, or the mule kicked him? All the possible tragedies raced through her head. *Perhaps he went out to find Haakan. Or over to Kaaren's.* As each place on her own homestead yielded no laughing little boy, she grew more desperate. Her heart thundered in her ears as she ran across the field to Kaaren's house.

"No, he's not here. I haven't seen him." Kaaren left the house and headed for their barn. "I'll look around here. Send Thorliff out for the men."

Oh, God, dear God, watch over my son. I failed to keep close watch on him. Please don't punish such an innocent child for the carelessness of his mother.

"Andrew, Andrew, where are you?" she called, her voice ringing out across the prairie. She called again. But there was no answering giggle. No "Mor, see me."

She ran to her husband, Haakan's arms as soon as he drove the team into the yard.

"When did you see him last?"

"When I put him down for his nap. I put up the bars, but he must have crawled over them or through them or something. Haakan, he is gone, and we cannot find him." She looked out across the waving grasses of the prairie, beyond the area immediately around the house and barn. The hay-fields stood knee-high again and beyond. A man could, and at times had, gotten lost in the sea of rippling grasses. If a man could get lost, how much more would a little boy be swallowed up.

"The river!" Suddenly remembering the river, Ingeborg wrenched herself from Haakan's arms and raced across the garden, heading for the meandering Red River.

"Ingeborg, wait!" Haakan tore the harness from Belle and leaped aboard. He swerved to miss the garden and galloped after the running woman. When he caught up with her, he pulled the horse to a halt and braced his foot for her to use as a step. "Come, get on." She put her foot on top of his and grasped his proffered hand. With a grunt, he swung her up behind him. "Has anyone sent for Metiz?"

"Baptiste went after her." Ingeborg scanned the ground, the grasses, the trees, but nowhere did she see any sign of the missing child.

They entered the trees at the road cleared for hauling wood and water, but before they reached the water's edge, Metiz waved them back. "He no here. I look." She waved up and down the river bank.

"How far could he get? He wasn't alone that long. Oh, how could I let him get lost like this?"

Dusk was falling by the time the neighbors arrived. Thorliff had taken Jack the mule and gone to tell the Baards and the others. Within each arriving wagon lay a pile of quilts and hides, lanterns and food. People brought whatever they had on hand, for no one knew how long the search would last.

Haakan sent groups out combing the fields and woods and the prairie grasses. Hours later, they returned empty-handed. No little boy in a calf-length shift accompanied them.

"We can't see anymore tonight, and the mosquitoes are driving everyone crazy," Joseph Baard, one of their best friends and closest neighbors said in an undertone to Haakan. "We'd best start again at dawn."

The mosquitoes, poor baby, the insects would be eating him alive—if he was still alive. Oh, God, I can't stand this. Where are you? Don't you care about my son?

One by one as the searchers returned, they ate a sandwich, drank some hot coffee or cold water, and fell asleep on whatever was handy, the ground, the haystacks, wagon beds.

"What are you doing?" Haakan laid a hand on Ingeborg's shoulder.

She shrugged him off. "I'm lighting a lantern, what does it look like? I will go look again. Surely if he hears my voice, he will answer."

"Where will you go? Do you think you can see better than all the others?"

"No, but maybe they frightened him, their strange voices and all. Maybe he's hiding, too afraid to come out." She slid the glass chimney in place on the lantern. "Oh, Haakan, he's all alone out there. I want my baby" Her voice broke as he took her in his arms and held her close.

"I know, I know." When she quieted, he tipped her chin up with gentle fingers. "Promise me you won't go out tonight. Your lantern could go out, and we could lose you too. Please, it isn't long until dawn, and then we will begin the search again. One thing to be grateful for—it isn't cold, so he won't freeze to death."

"Ja, but it might rain." She glanced up at the starless sky. "Oh, what if he's caught in the rain?"

"Ingeborg, listen to me. We prayed for Lars' foot and God healed him. Would He do less for our beloved son?"

"Sometimes God doesn't answer prayers like that. I should know." The pit of despair yawned before her, threatening to suck her into its whirling depths as it had before. "If I lose Andrew, I know I shall lose my mind."

"Oh, Inge, no. We are one now, you and me. We are stronger together. You don't have to bear this alone. I am here, and God never left."

Ingeborg raised her lantern and blew it out. The yard fell dark, the wind blew, and the howl of a hunting coyote could be heard in the distance. She shuddered and wrapped her arms around her sides. "You go sleep, if you can. Tomorrow, or rather today, may be the longest day of our lives."

"Inge—"

"No, I need to be alone now." She listened as he made his way back to the house. He wouldn't find a bed there, she knew. Someone else had already usurped that soft surface.

She wandered around the barn listening to the sheep, restless at the coyote's song. Were the wild animals finding a new kind of prey? *Oh, God, please keep my child safe.* Metiz hadn't returned either. Was she far up the river searching? A little one like Andrew would drown so easily. Why hadn't she taught him to swim? The whys drove her around to the corral. The horses slumbered, the hogs snorted in their sleep. All appeared peaceful, but for a small child lost in the miles of never ending prairie grass.

She sank down on the washstand at the side of the house. "Oh, God, how can I bear this" *My grace is sufficient for thee.* The verse stole softly through her mind, followed by another, *Lo, I am with you always,* and bits of another. She leaned her head against the rough slabs of dry sod and swatted a mosquito away. They seemed to come in swarms, their whine louder than the wind singing through the grasses.

Behold, I am thy God… The Lord is my Shepherd. "Dear God, tend your little wandering lamb tonight." She breathed in the stillness, redolent with the smells of a summer night. The roses sent their fragrance wafting around the corner, the earth damp with dew, the moisture of a storm in the distance, all part and parcel of their land. But where was Andrew?

Slowly the sky lightened, so faintly at first she thought she might be imagining it. But the band in the east brightened and broadened, giving promise of the returning sun. She could hear someone bustling around inside the sod house, the clank of stove lids, the thud of wood.

The sky lightened further, chasing the clouds so a few stars directly above glittered in their perfect splendor. Far away, beyond time and help—like God. She shook her head. *No, I will not go back to that. God is here and now, as He says He is.* She stumbled to her feet and followed the path to the outhouse. On her return, with their dog Paws padding beside her, she walked around the barn and looked to the south, to the prairie grasses bending before the breeze, illuminated with the dawn.

The prairie. It hadn't broken her before. It wouldn't break her now. *As God holds my hand,* she promised the flat land, *you will not break me.* She shook her fist at the rising sun as it painted the few remaining clouds in shades of purple, lavender, and pink. "You will not!"

She retrieved a hayfork from the barn and began forking hay from the middle stack into the sheep pen. Today, no one would take them out to graze. They would all look for Andrew. But no matter what despair shattered the human heart, the animals still had to be fed and watered.

Paws yipped and streaked out across the pasture just south of the barn. Ingeborg stabbed her fork into the stack and wandered around to see what had excited the dog.

Stumbling across the stubble, a hand buried in the hair of the gray wolf padding slowly beside him, the little lost child arrived home.

"Andrew!" Ingeborg screamed his name and flew across the ground separating them. "Thank you, God, thank you, thank you." She babbled as she ran toward her son, and the tears she'd been too terrified to shed poured down her face. The wolf sat, and Andrew ran to her on his own. She swept him up in her arms, hugging him as though she'd never let him go again. "Oh, Andrew, An- drew, thank God, you are safe!"

"Mor, big dog." He pointed back to the wolf, who sat panting quietly. "No, Andrew. That is Wolf, Metiz' Wolf. He is our friend."

"Big dog," Andrew insisted. "Mange takk, Wolf."

The animal blinked and faded back, disappearing into the morning mist just as Haakan ran across the field to stand beside her.

"Was that really a wolf?"

Ingeborg nodded. "Metiz' Wolf."

"And he brought Andrew back?"

"Ja, he did." Ingeborg kissed her son's filthy cheek and brushed her hand over the welts on his face and arms caused by a myriad of mosquito bites. "Uff da, so terrible you are bitten."

Haakan stared at the space where the big gray Wolf had been. "Well, I'll be. God surely used a strange way to protect our son."

Our son, how good that sounded.

"Mor, me hungry." The little one shook his head. "No Tor, Mor."

"You think he went hunting for Thorliff?" Haakan reached over to carry the boy, who went right into his arms.

"No doubt." Together they entered the yard where all the rescuers waited.

"Praise God, He saved our boy." Agnes called from the door, "Food's on, folks. Come eat, and then you can all go home and do your chores."

"The good Lord saved our boy" Haakan pointed to the east. "just in time to see a new day rising." He put his other arm around Ingeborg's waist.

"Praise God, indeed." She felt the strength of the man beside her, one more thing to be thankful for.

"Mor, I hungry."

"So, let's get some food in you, little one." Haakan carried the child through the crowd of well- wishers, who shook the man's hand and patted the child on his back or on his cheek.

Ingeborg watched them go, the tears still streaming unnoticed down her face. God certainly did provide in an unusual way. But then, didn't He always? During all the heartache of the last four years, all the deaths, the body-breaking labor, God had been there all the time, when she turned to look for Him. And now with all the joys, friends, family, crops, a child found, He was here, too, all the time. And He would not leave them. As Haakan said, this was surely a new day rising.

"Mor, you're crying," Thorliff said at her elbow.

"I know, but these are tears of joy, from a heart overflowing with thanksgiving." She laid a hand on his shoulder.

Thorliff shook his head. "Be easier just to say mange takk."

Made in the USA
Coppell, TX
30 September 2020